Alien: Betrayal

by

Tony Bradman

Illustrated by Nigel Dobbyn

First published in 2009 in Great Britain by
Barrington Stoke Ltd
18 Walker St, Edinburgh, EH3 7LP

www.barringtonstoke.co.uk

ISBN: 978-1-84299-699-7

Printed in Great Britain by Bell & Bain Ltd

A Note from the Author

I love science fiction and war stories. Best of all are science fiction stories that are about wars – tales of alien invasions and humans who fight back, or battles in space. I thought it would be fun to write a story like that. So I wrote *Alien*, the first book in this trilogy.

Alien introduced Jake, a human boy soldier caught up in an endless war. Jake met an alien girl, Tala, who was supposed to be his enemy – but he found out she wasn't. Now, in the second book, *Alien: Betrayal*, we meet Jake and Tala again. Someone's betrayed them, and they're both in danger. Read on to see where their story takes them ...

For the boys –
Hayden, Mark, Oscar, Tom

Contents

Chapter 1

Rubbish Boys

"You know, Tiny, I'll never get used to it," Jake said with a sigh. He was in a large room, standing by the doorway with a spade over his shoulder. The walls were made of concrete. There were harsh strip lights high overhead and no windows in the bunker.

"Get used to what, Jake?" said Tiny, the boy beside him. Tiny was huge, a lot bigger than other boys of his age. He had a big spade over his shoulder, too.

"The smell," said Jake, holding his nose. "The whole place stinks."

Jake nodded at the great pile of rubbish in front of them. The proper name for the room was Waste Disposal Centre Five. Rubbish was taken here from all over the underground bunker. The boys had to put it down a hole

into a chute in one of the walls. No one knew where it went after that. No one cared.

The only other thing in the room was a News Screen. There was one in almost every part of the bunker. The Old Ones liked to tell people what was going on in the war, so the screens were on the whole time. But these days Jake tried to block out the grim voices and awful pictures.

He sighed again, but soon he and Tiny were hard at work. The rubbish was mostly empty food ration packs, crushed drinks cans and scraps of rotting food. But there were uniforms as well, blackened and torn apart by laser beams and stained with blood ...

That's where the smell comes from, thought Jake. *It's the stink of death. Each uniform was worn by a soldier who died in this war. A kid like me or Tiny, made to fight by The Old Ones, while they stayed safe in the bunker.*

"I still can't believe one of the squad told on us," said Tiny. "Have you worked out who it was?"

"Not yet," said Jake with a frown. "But I will."

Jake put down his spade and wiped the sweat from his face. A few weeks ago he had been a Squad Leader on the front line. He had led ten soldiers, the best on planet Earth, people he could trust. Or at least he had thought so ...

They were kids, of course, like him and Tiny. The war had started many years ago when a race of aliens called the Krell had arrived on Earth. Most of the grown-ups had been killed – so the kids were left to do the fighting.

Some of the grown-ups who were still alive were in charge. They were called The Old Ones, and they said the Krell were evil. But one night on a mission, Jake had met an alien girl called Tala – and had found out that was a lie.

I tried to do what we agreed, Tala, Jake thought. *I tried to tell people that the war should stop. But someone in my squad betrayed me to The Old Ones, and they sent me here to punish me. So now we're rubbish boys, Tiny and me ...*

Suddenly the News Screen got louder. "Reports are coming in that a Krell Night Scout has been captured ..." said the excited news-reader.

Jake glanced at the screen and saw an alien being dragged into the bunker. There were the long arms and legs that all the aliens had and the big golden eyes. But then Jake looked more closely – it was Tala!

Chapter 2

Badly Beaten

Jake knew it was her – he would know that gentle face anywhere. She was being held by two members of the State Guards, the last few adult soldiers. Their job was to protect The Old Ones – and they were brutal.

They threw Tala down onto the concrete floor. One of them kicked her, and she lay there moaning. *It looks as if she's been badly beaten already*, Jake thought. *And those two thugs are posing for the camera, standing over her with their laser rifles held high and big grins on their ugly faces ...*

A young News Screen reporter hurried up to speak to them.

"So this is one of the famous Krell Night Scouts," she said. "Well, she doesn't seem so

scary now, does she? Can you tell us how she was captured?"

"There was a fire fight in Sector 13," said one of the guards. "And we killed the rest of her troops ..."

"Oh, yeah?" muttered Tiny, glaring at the screen. "I bet it was kids who did the fighting. I expect you took her from them so you could grab the glory!"

"Shut up," Jake snapped. "I'm trying to listen. This is important!"

"And what will happen to her now, then?" the young reporter asked.

"We're taking her to see The Old Ones," the second Guard said with pride. "They'll want to question her."

"And somehow I don't think the Krell's going to have a *long* life, do you?" said the first Guard. The two of them laughed.

Jake watched as the Guards dragged Tala off. She looked scared, but still ready to fight back. Jake clenched his fists, trying to control his anger and fear for his friend. *Her whole squad wiped out! And The Old Ones are cruel – they'll torture her before they kill her. How can those thugs make a joke about such a terrible thing?*

After a while Jake felt Tiny's hand on his arm. "It's her, isn't it, Jake? She's the Krell girl you met that night, the one you told us about."

"Got it in one, Tiny," said Jake. "We have to save her."

"Whoa, hang on a moment ..." said Tiny. "How?"

"Good question," said Jake. "I'll have to come up with a plan."

"That won't be a problem for you," said Tiny.

Jake turned to smile at him. Tiny was a gentle giant who fought like a demon. He could hack into any computer, too, however strong its fire-walls. They had been together for a long time, and Jake was sure Tiny

hadn't been the betrayer ... Suddenly Jake
had a fantastic idea.

"I think I've just come up with one of my
best," Jake told Tiny.

A plan to kill two birds with one stone, he
thought. *If it works, that is...*

Chapter 3

Suicide Mission

There weren't many places to have a secret meeting, but Jake and Tiny knew the perfect one, a store room no one used. Half an hour later, they were waiting in there.

"Are you sure they're coming?" said Jake. He was marching up and down, afraid of what they might be doing to Tala. They didn't have much time.

"Relax, Jake," said Tiny. "I texted them, and they've all texted me back. The whole squad will be here. But I'm still not sure it's such a great idea."

"Well, I am," said Jake, grinning at him. "So you'll just have to trust me."

I expect Tiny must think I'm mad to get the squad together again and tell them my plan to save Tala, he thought. *Most of all*

when we don't know which one is the traitor.
But what better way to find out who that
person is?

Just then, two kids walked into the store
room. They were wearing the uniforms of
soldiers, although they only looked ten or
eleven.

"Hey, Katie and Shofiq!" said Jake,
grinning. "Good to see you!" Katie and
Shofiq grinned too, and soon the others
arrived. There were Joe and Dan and Sarah,
who had been made a squad leader. There

20

were Maria and Polly and Wicksy. And there was Alfie, a good kid to have beside you in a fire fight.

Jake watched them while they talked. The squad had been split, each kid sent to a different part of the army, so they had plenty of catching up to do. *I bet The Old Ones made them say nothing about my message of peace*, Jake thought. *They let me and Tiny stay together – and that was their biggest mistake. I know the rest of the squad was on my side too – all of them except the one who betrayed me.*

21

Jake saw Tiny looking at him over the heads of the others. He raised his eye-brows as if to ask whether Jake had worked out who the betrayer was yet. Jake gave a tiny shake of his head.

"OK, listen up, guys," he said. "Did any of you see the news report about the Krell Night Scout who was captured today? It was on the screens about an hour ago."

Some of them muttered that they had, while others simply nodded their heads. Most looked puzzled.

"Well, that was Tala, the Krell girl I told you about," said Jake. The kids all looked at each other, eyes wide. "And I'm going to get her out of the prison block. But I won't be able to do it without your help ..."

Suddenly they were excited, and everyone started to speak at once.

"We're with you, Jake!" said Alfie at last. "Tell us what we have to do!"

"You might not like it once you hear my plan," said Jake. "It's very simple. But for

24

some of us it could turn out to be a suicide mission."

"That's OK," said Alfie. "I'm on kitchen duty, so I'm already bored to death."

The rest of them grinned in a nervous way. Jake nodded. *So far, so good*, he thought.

Chapter 4

Attack Squad

"Right, this is what we're going to do," said Jake, looking round at them. "First we break into the Weapons Room to get some laser rifles. Then we free Tala."

"But the Guards are holding her," said Sarah. "And they'll shoot to kill."

"So will we," said Jake. "That's why we need the lasers. We'll hit the prison block hard and fast. And we're the best attack squad there is, aren't we, guys?"

"Oh yeah!" yelled most of the squad. But Sarah shook her head.

"I know it seems crazy, Sarah," said Jake. "And I know we've all had a hard time. But we can't let The Old Ones kill Tala. She's trying to stop this war, and she'd do the same for any one of us. She saved me, remember?"

"Have it your way," Sarah said with a shrug.

Jake looked at her ... then went on to explain his plan. "Now you all know what to do. We'll split up and each of us will make our own way to the Weapons Room. Check your watches, everyone. We'll meet there in 20 minutes, OK?"

The squad left one by one, and Jake just hoped that none of them would get hurt because of what he was doing. *The betrayer must think I'm stupid. Splitting the squad up like this means he or she can go and tell The Old Ones about my plan ... But that's the most important part of the whole thing.*

Tiny was going to leave with the rest, but Jake held him back. "Hang on, Tiny," he said. "I've got a job just for you. I'd like you to hack into the bunker's main computer and find out where that rubbish chute goes to."

"No problem," said Tiny. He dug into the huge pocket of his trousers and pulled out a small old laptop. "Do you want anything else while I'm at it?"

"Nice of you to ask," said Jake. "It might be useful if you could mess up the system a bit."

Tiny grinned. Soon his huge fingers were clicking over the laptop's key-board ...

20 minutes later, Jake and Tiny were at the door of the Weapons Room. The whole squad was behind them, with Alfie and Maria keeping watch at the back. The door was locked, and Tiny got to work on the keypad.

Suddenly there was a click and the door hissed open. Jake led the squad in. The walls of the room were lined with racks that held dozens of laser guns. There were boxes of ammo, and stun grenades as well.

"OK, guys, take what you need," said Jake. "Then let's get out of here!"

Jake grabbed a rifle for himself, and looked at his watch. *Time is running out for Tala*, he thought ...

31

Suddenly there was a flash from outside and a laser beam sizzled over the heads of the squad. "Drop your guns," yelled a voice. "You're under arrest!"

Chapter 5

A Big Surprise

Five State Guards charged into the
Weapons Room and aimed their rifles at the
squad. Tiny and Alfie raised their own rifles,
but Jake knew it was a waste of time. *We'd
all be wiped out before we could even pull
our triggers*, he thought. *They've got us
covered. They'd enjoy killing us, too.*

"Hold your fire, everyone!" he said. "But don't put down your weapons."

"Don't listen to him," said a different voice.

The Old Ones came into the room, three of them, two men and a woman. Jake had seen Old Ones before, of course, but he could never get over just how odd they looked. They had silver hair and wore long, flowing, golden robes.

It had been the woman who had spoken. Now she stood staring at Jake.

"Do you think I should fall on my knees and beg you to forgive me or something?" he said. "You should know me better than that."

"Oh, we know you well, Jake," said the woman, smiling. "And we know about your plan to free our prisoner. You can't hide anything from us."

"That's only because you get us kids to spy on each other," said Jake. "Someone in my squad has betrayed me twice now."

"But it can't be true!" said Alfie. "None of us would do that, Jake ..."

Most of the squad spoke at once, claiming that they had never betrayed Jake.

"Shut up, all of you!" said the woman. "There's no point in hiding it any more. You're right, Jake. A member of your squad has been keeping us informed about you. But it wasn't betrayal, she was just being a good girl. Come out here ... Sarah."

There were gasps from the squad as Sarah walked across and stood in front of The Old Ones. The woman put her hands on Sarah's shoulders.

"Traitor!" yelled Alfie. "How could you do it after everything we've been through together?"

"I think I can guess," said Jake. *I had a feeling she was the one*, he thought. "You

always wanted to be a squad leader, didn't you? And betraying me was the fastest way to get to the top."

"It was a better bet than waiting for you to get killed," said Sarah with a smile. "It didn't matter what was going on, you always seemed to come out of it alive."

"I can see how cross that must have made you," said Jake, and looked at his watch. *Only a few more seconds to go,* he thought. *Someone's in for a big surprise ...*

"It's time we put an end to your evil plans for good, Jake," said the woman with a frown. "You'll have to die. So will the rest of you, I'm afraid. We don't want any witnesses. Guards – kill them!"

Suddenly the lights went out and the room was plunged into total darkness.

"Squad – take cover!" yelled Jake. The Guards fired. Laser beams crackled and zipped through the gloom. But the squad knew what to do, and soon they were firing back. They forced the Guards to retreat with

the three Old Ones and Sarah. "Well done, Tiny!" Jake said. "I knew I could count on you!"

That was the easy part, thought Jake. *Now we have to free Tala ...*

Chapter 6

Alarm Bells

They fought their way out of the Weapons Room just in time. As they left, a shot from the Guards hit a crate of grenades and blew the room apart.

"Quick, this way!" yelled Jake. He led his squad down a passage that was filled with

smoke. A few moments later he held his hand up and they halted.

"Wow, that was close," muttered Alfie. "What's the plan, Jake?"

"Thanks to Tiny, the bunker is going to be a very confusing place for everyone except us. Just how long have we got, Tiny?" asked Jake.

"10 minutes, 15 at the most," said Tiny, with a shrug. "It will take them that long to re-boot the main computer and get the lights back on."

"That should give us plenty of time," said Jake, looking round at the keen faces of his squad. "Tiny and me will head for the prison block," he said. "I want the rest of you to cause as much confusion as possible."

"We can do that," said Alfie, grinning.

"I'm sure you can," said Jake. "We'll meet you at Waste Disposal Centre Five in

15 minutes. And make sure none of you gets hurt, OK?"

Jake and Tiny ran through the dark passages of the bunker. Soon they could hear laser fire and explosions and alarm bells clanging behind them. They hurried on, and came at last to the door of the prison block. Two State Guards were waiting for them – the same two who had boasted about capturing Tala.

There was a fire fight. Laser beams sizzled all over the place. But the boys were tough fighters who knew what they were doing, and the thugs didn't have a chance. A few seconds later, Jake and Tiny stepped over their bodies and made for Tala's cell.

"Stand back, Tala!" he yelled. He hung a grenade on the door handle and pulled the pin. "Fire in the hole!" he yelled, and he and Tiny ducked down.

There was a dull boom and the door flew off. Then they saw a well-known shape appear through the smoke. Tala smiled at her human friend, her golden eyes gleaming.

"It seems it's your turn to save me this time, Jake," she said.

Jake was glad he'd found her before she had been tortured. She was black and blue from the beating she'd been given, but she seemed OK.

The rest of the squad were waiting for them when they arrived at Waste Disposal Centre Five. They all said hello to Tala, who nodded in a shy way. Suddenly the lights came on and Jake ordered everyone over to the chute.

"Right, this is our escape route," he said. "Tiny has found out that it leads to the deserted old city. And once we're there The Old Ones will never find us."

I just wish it wasn't so smelly, thought Jake as he climbed into the chute after Tiny. *I'll have to make sure The Old Ones find out how awful it is when I come back ...*

Jake crept on through the dark tunnel and out into the daylight of the old city. The future was bright.

Barrington Stoke would like to thank all its readers for commenting on the manuscript before publication and in particular:

Tia Bodkin
Brandon Booth
Hussana Bostan
Stephen Brown
Liam Buttress
Jaswantie Darchiville
Martin Darchiville
Emily Eminson
Bradley Fell
Joshua Gamble
Meena Hadiy
C. Jones
Sumina Kasuji
Daniella Lee
Maria Loftus
Keeley Maycock
Rayhan Mohammed
Bènèdicte de Rancourt
Tia Read
Catherine Smith
Ky Stringer
Annum Yaqoob

Become a Consultant!

Would you like to give us feedback on our titles before they are published? Contact us at the email address below – we'd love to hear from you!

info@barringtonstoke.co.uk
www.barringtonstoke.co.uk

More gr8reads from Barrington Stoke

**Alien
by
Tony Bradman**

The world at war!
The aliens are attacking!
Everyone must fight.
But just who is the
enemy?

**Hornet
by
Chris Powling**

Hornet's an outlaw.
A killer.
The best shot in the Wild
West.
And he has a score to
settle with Gil ...

You can order these books directly from our website at
www.barringtonstoke.co.uk

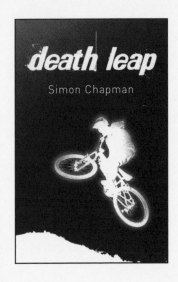

**Death Leap
by
Simon Chapman**

Jake saw a murder.
The killers saw Jake.
Now the killers are after
him ...

**Liar
by
Pete Johnson**

Dave lied to save
himself.
Now it's war – and
things are really out of
control ...

You can order these books directly from our website at
www.barringtonstoke.co.uk